TOSHIRO BURNING

Gary David Springer

CONTENTS

The Waking Dream   1

Waking   3

Shedding   4

Splitting   5

Mission   6

Climb to Cotopaxi   7

Landing   9

Slipping   10

Caravan   12

Choosing   14

Lahar   17

Unwelcome   20

Ash of the Amazon   23

Invitation   25

Corazón   27

Sangre de Drago   30

Quake and Flood   33

Hazel   35

Fever   37

Flight   39

Stories   41

Flicker   43

Cutting   46

Jun   48

Rubble   50

Orders   52

The Atacama   55

Koi   57

Crash   60

Testing   63

Amber Sun   67

Rust   70

Paranal   73

Silence   75

Wasteland   77

Bronze   80

Circling   83

Every Skin   85

Debt and Duty   91

Warnings   96

Monks and Rangers   99

Razor   101

Monje   103

Machina   106

Coyotes and Slavers   110

Sunset Glow   113

Best of Men   118

Trust   122

Sheaves   125

Teachers   131

Brief Bend   135

Fingers and Thumb   138

Dreams   141

Antonio   147

El Cabro   149

El Potro   152

Obsidian   157

Pachamama   160

Penitentes   163

Tribes   167

Prayers   170

Night March   173

Secret   177

Shards   179

Healing   183

Blind   185

Statue   186

Southern End   189

The Eel   191

Kingdoms   194

Red Tide   197

The Gulf 200

Pod 202

Mother and Calf 207

Fjords 209

Turbines 212

Bodhi 215

Butterflies 222

Pappus 225

South 230

Valientes 235

Black 239

Free 242

The Waking Dream

Waking

I,
Toshiro,
wake on the sea.

I blink
under darkening sky.

The sea climbs high
in boiled mists and steaming airs.

The winds spin white and grey
in tempest spiral.

The lifted waves
crash low in sheets –
a grey-white, sharp-beaked flock.

Our floating city heaves,
bobs,
groans.

But the domes never crack.

The links of the cells hold strong.

<u>Shedding</u>

The spent storm tires
into a calm and flattened sea.

We cross the
bright Ocean of Peace.

Our city sheds its cells
like petals from the flower.

Back,
the seasteads drift -
a long and winding chain.

Farmers drop the substrate bones,
anxious eyes to the sky.

By the Islands of Darwin,
all petals have been shed.

Only the core remains.

The woman
with hair of silver
beckons with two fingers.

<u>Splitting</u>

We talk on the bridge of the ship,
bronze shirts all around,
tapping at their screens.

She points to another bridge –
a twin across the core:

Look, Toshiro,
there is not one ship here,
but two.

The twin bridge moves.

Away.

We slide deeper into the sea.

Now, I understand:
Our core was not a circled disc,
but two mantas interwoven.

Tail slides over tail.

The twin rays part.

Mission

The sun falls swiftly behind us,
dies in embers red and violet.

We chase the dawn
through black-hazed night.

The manta slices
from wave to wave,
gliding free,
a creature of both
sea and air.

Firefly drones light our way
with flickering crests,
gold-pooled troughs.

The woman's eyes shine silver, too,
though weary in the night:

Toshiro,
born of the East,
will travel the South.

Toshiro, my child,
will journey the length
of the Andean spine.

Climb to Cotopaxi

<u>Landing</u>

Seven times
we cruise the coast
from the Canal to Esmeraldas.

But the shoreline never welcomes.

Mosquito planes,
dark and missile-winged,
swarm above the cities.

Warships chase us
far from the tide plants,
their cannons raised, turrets swinging,
mistaking us for pirates.

We wait for new storm.

When a black fog billows,
we ride below.

When the front drives deep,
we slip like shadow onto shore.

And from the manta's mouth
we pour upon the sand:
light trucks,
small transports,
jeeps like beetles
ribcage bare.

Slipping

Through coastal towns we drive.

We avoid the many soldiers of the Bishop –
the machine-gun paladins
of camouflage and black cross.

They stand like tired oaks in guard
of barracks, banks, and churches.

They roam the plazas and the markets,
collecting the Bishop's heavy tax
and strong-suggested tithe.

We look away from
their silver-glassed stare.

We slip beyond
the paved road's end
into the villages of box and tarp,
the dens of peddlers without permit.

Speaking little,
listening long,
we trade batteries
for straw chupallas,
tire-tread sandals,
poncho rain slickers
green and grey.

We search village after village,
looking for our screen.

And in the fourth we find our cover.

We see full beards, blond hair.

We hear cutting phrases
Dutch and German.

They are scientists
bound for the mountain:
trembling, smoldering
Cotopaxi.

Caravan

The caravan climbs
through the night.

We form a
lighted serpent chain
scaled red and white.

We weave through the hills.

Sengai drives,
his free hand stroking
grey-wisp beard like cat.

Sengai pauses in his stroking,
swerves to miss the work of mudslides:
rocks, shrubs, and branches
washed across the road.

The serpent of light climbs on,
red to its mouth,
white to its tail.

In an open stretch of road,
Sengai glances over,
widens eye.

Sengai questions:

What do you remember from the sea, Toshiro?

I answer:

> *I remember the storm.*

Sengai tests:

> *And before the storm?*

> *And before the sea?*

I cannot answer.

Sengai,
knowing,
nods,
strokes slow.

I stare at the rail,
the long drop into void.

Choosing

Sleepless,
I sit upon
a bluff.

Sengai,
sleepless,
joins me.

The night moves on
like river.

A moon of crescent silver
climbs.

Sometimes,
the moon shines
sharp and clear
through open voids.

Sometimes,
behind dark clouds,
the crescent blurs and dims -
a swollen, mist-burned arch.

At dawn,
the crescent thins;
the silver moon pales grey.

Tremors jar the mountain.

A pebbled rain falls from
bluff to base camp.

The little tents pack up.

The Europeans climb,
higher, deeper, nearer Cotopaxi.

The Asians flee
the waking mountain.

Sengai tests:

Who should we follow, Toshiro?

I answer:

*We should stay with our people,
our team.*

Sengai presses:

But why are we here?

I answer,
remembering her words at sea:

To see.

To learn.

To help.

Sengai,
nodding,
looks high to the
trembling mountain:

And who needs help?

*Those near or far
from danger?*

We hurry down the bluff,
climb the higher trail.

Lahar

Afoot,
we round
the base of
the mountain.

The German leads,
Sengai at her side.

I plod behind,
toting tools and gear.

We three
walk the ring
of seismic stations.

The stations are small:
little helmets on the rocky ground,
black visors dulled grey by fallen ash,
like samurai buried in basalt,
kabuto eyes to summit.

The German lifts plates,
checks sensors,
calls for tools.

Sengai wipes the ash,
cleans the inner lenses.

I run tools,
stumbling when
the mountain shivers.

We walk the ring.

The German works
without an upward gaze.

At the final station,
Sengai asks:

> *Do you not fear the mountain?*

The German, shrugging, answers:

> *Paxi is just dreaming now,*
> *tossing, turning.*

> *I will show you how he wakes.*

The German leads us to a plateau ridge.

She points up to
the whitened summit,
to a wide and dark fissure
through the glacier crown.

Her finger traces down
the deep-gouged furrow.

Down a jagged channel
midway fanning.

Down a riverbed dry
with black-melt stone.

And over the broad alluvial fan,
through shredded brush and mudded stones,
the legs of puma, fox, and deer
protrude.

Unwelcome

The Dutchman,
leader of the team,
summons us to base camp.

He takes us inside
a circled tent like Mongol yurt.

He questions us with answers:

>   *You came from the Isle of Edo.*

>   *You crossed the sea by floating city.*

>   *You are servants of the Okono Twins.*

The head of Sengai
slightly dips, slightly rises.

The Dutchman passes tables,
enters the core of the tent,
motions us to follow.

We move, silent,
to the edge of the void.

With single touch,
a wafer pops from the Dutchman's temple
by pole of magnet flipped,
repelling.

From his black webbed belt,
he changes the wafer of smooth jade
for a disk of striate pearl.

The Dutchman questions on,
his temple glowing:

You come to survey, no?

To survey and report?

Tell the Twins
that no one here
asks for their help.

Warn them:

The South is a
dangerous place.

The Dutchman disappears.

The empty tent core fills
with the Andes:

Diaphanous slopes grey and brown.

Glacier lakes of cerulean glass.

An emerald bed translucent.

And the deep earth dark and turning.

The Dutchman reappears as
a single point of light
over Cotopaxi.

Many lights appear
over the mountains.

One by one,
they speak.

At each report,
red magma boils higher
from the mantle,
seeps through cracks,
spews from cones.

Ash of the Amazon

Invitation

An orange-bearded scientist
follows us from the base tent.

He looks at us with jaundice eyes.

He speaks through wheezing breath:

> *Friends,*
> *you must understand.*
>
> *The Okonos*
> *are resented by many*
> *around the world.*
>
> *They are resented and feared*
> *and, sometimes, hated.*
>
> *Their thriving cities of the sea*
> *embitter the landborn sick and starving.*
>
> *It is said that*
> *she cares more for*
> *Synths than Humans;*
> *he builds great arch and prism towers,*
> *while closing gates to the refugees.*
>
> *In their naïve youth,*
> *they worked and dealt with warlord snakes.*

Now, twice burned,
the Twins withdraw from every conflict,
more neutral than the Swiss.

The scientist, wheezing, breathes from mask.

He leads us from the tent,
to a wide stone shelf,
a copter pad.

He lowers his mask,
points to the east, far beyond the mountain.

He speaks with raw-throat voice:

The tiltprop
leaves tomorrow
for Yasuni.

Come see the dying jungle with me.

Come and breathe the inland air.

Corazón

We ride upon the jungle clouds,
the billows turning thick and slow,
dark grey smoke more black than white,
with tails of orange like first-sparked fire.

At the sight of war planes in the east,
we plunge below the smoky clouds.

We level in the lighter haze.

And see a jungle without heart.

There is no forest here
save scattered groves and copses:
islands of green in a deadened sea.

Swaths of barren ash
separate the isles.

Riverbeds,
dry and trickling,
snake between.

We pass above
a yellow-bleached plain
of scrub and brush,
a bony herd
of pale white cattle.

We pass a town
of treeless ranches,
smokehouse sheds,
killing pens red-mudded.

Flying further,
the scientist sweeps his arm
across a broad scorched field to the south.

The parts of long-dead drones
litter the field:
charred antennae, wings, and legs,
overgrown with weeds;
abdomen shells split and cracked;
mangled thoraces, steel fangs embedded deep.

The scientist lowers his mask:

*The War of
Wasp and Spider.*

Araña y Arispa.

The Bishop lost.

Jefito won.

A petro plant,
abandoned,
lies center of the wreckage.

Dark pipes stretch tall
from rusty towers,
the black ground bare
of any weed.

    Jefito's prize.

Sangre de Drago

An emerald island nears,
a jungle wood still dense and lush,
a surviving patch of the ancient forest.

Mist-catchers ring the grove:
single-stilted towers.

As our tiltprop banks,
the gusts raise pennants from the towers,
long cones that fill with air.

And from each tower's base,
many driplines branch,
stretching deep into the forest.

A hut appears at the forest's edge,
a silver dome of solar sheets,
a mount of mirrored facets.

We land beside the hut.

We unload crates and boxes.

Sengai drips with sweat,
slaps mosquitoes,
fights for breath
in the heat.

A hundred eyes watch from the forest.

Young girls swing from the dragon trees.

Boys carve crescents in the scaly trunks,
soon to seep dark crimson.

The Guarani,
patient,
wait.

They emerge only
when we climb midsky.

Quake and Flood

Hazel

On our return,
the mountain spews
black ash in steady stream.

High winds smear the ash
like a dampened brush through drop of ink.

The rising plumes turn grey.

South,
we head
from Cotopaxi.

Up and down the hills,
we trail the laden trucks
of barley and potato.

Sengai tires in the night.

Open-mouthed,
he sleeps.

I drive by neural helm,
hands free.

The vulcan mountains shake.

Lightning splinters,
hazel,
white.

A clay rain falls.

Then sleet.

Then hail,
soon boiled.

I remember first storm on the sea.

Her voice returns,
light clear:

> *Find candles, Toshiro,*
> *kind flames in the night.*

<u>Fever</u>

Sengai,
pale,
shivers,
sweats.

I summon the map.

The South appears in crystalline light,
white, blue, and green.

I ask for the other teams' tracks.

A river bright red
flows from north to south.

The river branches into many streams.

The thin streams
cross, wind, weave,
down the Andean spine,
veering pass to pass.

The Medics lead all streams.

But their stream stops abruptly
in the Santa Valley,
where the flooding river
bends toward sea.

I set a course for the flooded valley.

The eyes of Sengai,
empty slits,
stare high.

Confused by the
grey-black clouds,
he asks:

Toshiro, is it night or day?

<u>Flight</u>

The rocky hills have cracked
like ice beneath bear's paw.

White water rushes through the clefts.

Mists both rise and fall.

The climbing road cracks, too,
and warps and twists and bows.

Crag boulders drop
to the roadside edge
like a giant's shattered teeth.

Strewn gravel gathers into drifts.

Skulls of cobble roll.

Red lights rush
through the cloud of dust.

I brake.

I count the trucks ahead:
Ten before the tunnel.

I park.

I walk.

A riderless mule gallops by,
saddlebag dragging.

A dam worker runs,
his broken arm to chest,
bleeding hand on helmet.

A utility crew,
eyes white with panic,
carries their mud-soaked, lifeless member.

Many more pour from the tunnel mouth.

Most follow the road.

Some,
fearing flood,
climb high.

Some,
fearing quake,
crawl low.

Sengai calls my name.

He joins the line working
their way down the steep slope,
gripping wrist to wrist,
throwing belt over boulder,
coat over scarp.

Stories

We shelter
inside a cavern.

We pace the
shadowed cage.

No one speaks
as the sky blackens slow.

Fresh stones fall from above.

Below, the river swells and surges.

The hard chill of night
draws strangers into
a tightened huddle;
backs and shoulders press,
shivering arms wrap waist.

Only two avoid the huddle:
the fevered Sengai curled in corner,
and I, alone, in cavern mouth.

Stories carry
through the sleepless night,
stories of witness,
stories of loss.

The speaker confesses;
the people absolve.

A mason heard the coming flood
like the wail of a thousand goats' slaughter,
then abandoned his apprentice in trench.

An officer watched
his barracks dissolve, floor by floor,
his soldiers climb to the roof,
soon under.

A Quechua cook clung to a tree
floating through the market,
reached for two children,
caught only one.

I stare into the river below,
slow with mud,
thick with ice.

By morning light,
the river falls
and clears.

<u>Flicker</u>

Midday,
the huddle of survivors breaks.

I wave them close
to the cavern mouth.

I point down
to the flattened river,
now more stream than flood.

Their empty eyes
flicker with life.

Before descending,
each survivor covers
Sengai with donation:
purple shawls,
red woolen vests,
ponchos brown and grey.

The lips of Sengai
quiver.

Hand in hand,
the survivors crawl down
from the cavern mouth.

The mountain tremors
weaken through the day.

The highest clouds of the sky
bear ash, not rain,
their bellies set
like porridge curds.

A feeble half-light
blankets the land,
weak as eclipse;
every outline
blurs dim grey.

Rescue planes fly
up and down the river,
dropping supplies,
gathering wounded.

Small boats troll each bank.

Long wooden poles push
the dead ashore.

Sengai mumbles in the dark.

He tries to stand.

I run and catch him
by the shoulders.

I drag him,
limp,
to the cavern mouth.

His hair of white-streaked black
lies damp upon his head,
salt-crusted by the fever sweat.

He draws weak breath.

He glances to
the mountains,
the sky,
the river.

The eyes of Sengai,
hard and bitter,
turn to me.

With a hollow voice, he speaks:

> *Lucky Toshiro never tires,*
> *never hungers or thirsts,*
> *never ails.*
>
> *Mother Okono*
> *would be so proud.*

Cutting

As moonlight creeps
into the cavern,
Sengai vomits,
groans,
curses.

He casts off
his mound of ponchos and vests,
draws a knife from his belt.

Sengai pulls tight
his long-wisp beard,
slices clean.

He pulls and saws
his matted hair
by handfuls.

Smiling, finished,
he closes his eyes,
leans back against
the stony wall.

He speaks in bitter, wounded voice:

A human acts, Toshiro.

A human chooses
then suffers for the choice.

Sengai opens his dark eyes
in the moonlight,
leans close.

He speaks by
breath of crystal mist:

> *Tell me of your choices, Toshiro.*
>
> *Tell me of your life before the storm.*
>
> *Share with me a memory, Toshiro,*
> *a single moment of pleasure or pain,*
> *an image carved by feeling,*
> *in childhood or youth.*
>
> *Give me one, Toshiro,*
> *one memory before the storm.*

Shivering works through Sengai,
through hands to arms to chest.

I cover him in ponchos.

Then from the cavern mouth
I shout and cry,
until a yellow searchlight
blinds.

Jun

While Sengai heals in camp,
I help Jun.

I fetch bandages, splints, peroxide.

I bring food and water for the injured,
hot coffee and coca leaves for her.

Jun has not slept in days.

On breaks,
behind the tent,
she smokes with shaking fingers.

Her eyes have cracks of blood.

She asks me of our journey.

I tell her of the mountain quakes,
the plume of Cotopaxi,
the ashen rains.

When I mention our flight
to the jungle heart, her eyes sharpen;
the fever of Sengai explained,
she nods.

After smoking,
Jun comes close.

She studies my teeth,
my tongue,
my eyes.

Cold fingers
feel my throat.

She takes my hand,
turns the wrist,
traces veins and tendons.

Impressed, she says:

So real.

Rubble

Sengai rises
on the first night,
fever gone.

He finds us in the city.

Jun,
unbelieving,
stares.

She feels his neck and forehead,
studies teeth and tongue and eyes.

Jun,
knowing,
looks away.

In the final search for life,
survivors dig through the Huaraz rubble.

Trucks cruise slowly
through the brick-strewn lanes,
their tires crushing glass to powder.

Mounted searchlights
pan the rubble.

Bare-ribbed dogs
sniff crumbled walls,
race pile to pile.

We leverage slabs by iron bar.

We sift and stir by shovel.

We shine lights
into the unreachable voids,
call out long,
and listen.

A vendor is found,
his hand still clinging to cart,
faintly breathing.

A priest is found,
crushed by pine bough,
broken neck.

We move into the floodpath:
a broad and flattened plain.

We see the heart of Huaraz
levelled by the wall
of mud, ice, and water,
a half-dried concrete,
heavy as cement.

Nothing lives
in the floodpath,
only rat and fly.

Orders

The Bishop is coming to Huaraz.

His officers and soldiers claim
the ground of the Santa Valley;
his wasp drones take the air,
weaving soundless through the breeze.

Foreigners are noticed in the crowds,
questions asked – a circle closing.

Behind the tent,
Jun delivers new orders
from the Twins.

All skilled medics will remain
in the White Mountains,
helping wherever they can.

All others will flee to the coast,
to gather in seaside Barranca,
beneath the open-armed
statue of Christ.

We leave weary Jun,
dozing against a tentpole,
her dark eyes closed,
mouth slipping wide.

We find our old transport.

We flee through city and town.

The Atacama

<u>Koi</u>

The seaside Christ
is armless:
a warlord's jab
to Bishop.

Our ash-crusted jeeps
idle on the beach.

Our trucks and transports
park by the Savior's feet.

A seagull crosses
the half-moon.

Exposed,
we wait, with
wary eyes to land.

A few climb
the cannon-shattered arms,
scope the town and hill and road.

A dark cloud
swallows the moon.

Nothing
comes from land.

But,
behind,
the ocean opens.

A seacraft
outruns the tide.

It settles on the sand
like long beached koi.

The winged fins tilt
and drip black waters.

The mouth opens.

A ramp floats down.

The Twins appear
from the darkened belly,
their skin lit bright
by an unseen sun.

Phantom free,
they cross the beach
without a step.

Brother speaks first:

    All is speed now,
    brothers,
    sisters.

Riderless cycles
emerge from the mouth,
darker than shadow,
swallowing sound.

The cycles array on the beach,
morph two wheels to four.

Sister, urgent,
speaks:

Race to the desert mounts.

To the Atacama.

Crash

We ride a
slender strip of road
between the mountains
and the sea.

My cycle screen
warns, guides, prods...

weapons in passing cars
throb a crimson red;

branched paths weave through traffic,
the safest path flashing solid green,
the risky flickering yellow;

in open stretches,
the cycle motor flares,
strains like horse against the rein,
rests only in the sprint.

Sengai,
behind me,
is now ahead,
swift as jet's shadow.

I let him go.

I follow only the paths of safest green.

Another cycle streaks by,
bald Egan splitting trucks.

I wait and pass
by solid green.

Into a range of stony hills,
we ride.

The road climbs steep,
cuts east and west by
sudden bends.

Ahead,
a jeep throbs crimson,
its every rider armed.

I loose the engine.

I seize a dim-lit yellow lane
and pass on narrow corner.

Bend to bend,
I fly.

I climb,
full power.

The range plateaus.

The crooked straightens.

A black-dust cloud.

Blood on the road.

A mangled grey fox,
spine through fur.

Sengai cruises slowly
through the wreckage trail.

We stop at Egan's body.

The body,
road-flayed,
drips no blood
but little beads of
viscous silver fluid.

His bones,
unshattered,
strangely warp
and curl.

Sengai looks from
the lifeless Synth
to me.

I look away,
fly by.

Testing

Every rider stops
at the edge of the
boiling fields.

Long we stare in a fearful pack,
gauging danger, weighing choices.

Sulfur and ammonia
waft heavy through the air.

Hot mud slurries from
cones of dark clay.

Vulcan steams bore up
through the bedrock,
launch white vapor high
in crackling geysers.

Acid streams eat away stone
like Hadean rivers.

Our oldest rider,
a man of pale hair
and stooped shoulders,
points to distant Canabur,
the smoking mountain
high over the fields.

He speaks to the pack:

The pack talks.

The pack chooses.

Sengai touches my arm,
pulls me close,
speaks slow and clear:

You choose the way now, my friend.

Choose your path and mine.

I watch
cycle after cycle
cut to the south.

I gaze long at the
windblown black smoke
of the mountain,
the white rising steam
of the fields.

I answer Sengai
with words both
unsure and certain:

I will trust in the Twins.

The Brother must see
the wide world and
our future clear.

The Sister must plan
for the whole living Body,
from Human to Ant,
Moon to Star.

We ride for the
heart of the desert.

Only two riders join us.

A woman.

And girl.

Amber Sun

By night,
the hills pass
dead and grey.

Moonlight pales
on jagged ridgelines,
disappears in cavern hollows.

But the land burns red
by the rising sun.

Sandstone mounts
climb sheer into the cloudless sky,
their strata lit bright
scarlet,
coral, and
vermillion.

Furrowed by wind,
ochre dunes snake between the mounts,
rise in challenge of the firmer crests,
always spilling, tumbling short.

The noon sun paints
with driest amber.

Swaths copper and bronze
alternate through the broken hills.

Sienna powders,
sepia grains,
sands of burnt umber,
all crawl high between
the steep hill flanks.

The older drivers
fade with dusk.

Sengai nudges cliff walls,
scraping stone.

Sara lags,
drifts, wanders off.

We stop together.

We rest
our backs to
a citadel of stone.

The old drink deep,
slump lower on the wall.

Young Ichika points
to the candled river of stars -
violet, gold, emerald.

She asks of my birth
in the storm.

She tells of her own
on the sea:

The great mantas circled
the isle of prism and tower.

The gates opened slower than tide.

The Twins
led me by the hand
to the dock.

The Twins smiled proud.

They whispered to me
of great things I would do.

And the old servants glared
as we walked.

Rust

We follow paths of dust
carved by ancient rivers,
canyons and gorges
a million years dry.

The ground pales,
reddens,
flakes of rust
crumbled and bleached
by long sun.

The salt of dried seas
sprinkles the dunes like fresh snow;
white crystals vein the red hills,
drift in the clefts and ravines.

Canabur smokes.

Canabur trembles.

Stones roll low.

Sara swerves
from a stone
into dune.

Rushing,
we pry her leg free,
lift her up.

She walks a few limping steps.

Ichika scolds the older woman.

Sengai defends:

> *The stone rolled.*

> *What could she do?*

> *This journey is test —*
> *you to your limits,*
> *us far beyond.*

The Twins speak
from our screens.

We hurry to see them,
sit down in the cab.

The Okonos warn us that
much worse is coming.

Our screens blacken deep.

Darkness enters the sky.

Stars glisten,
sway.

The white suns flow slowly
like leaves in the stream.

The lights gather
in the southern sky,
funnel down in bright pillar.

To far Paranal,
to star-watching mount,
we are guided.

Paranal

Silence

We are ruined by our haste.

Each leading driver
stirs up great clouds of dust
in their wake.

The fine dust clogs every filter,
stiffens each joint,
coats every panel with
a grit paste like cement.

When the last cycle fails,
we load all the supplies we can carry.

We walk on in silence.

We march through the night.

Toward the pillar of stars,
white-blue in our goggles.

The straight path to the pillar
leads over dunes.

Then up and down hills.

Then through fields of rock.

We pass dark lagoons
without ripple or wave.

But the guiding pillar of stars
seems no closer.

We are committed now.

Too deep to turn back.

Through day's heat
we march.

The bright sun dims
grey in our goggles.

The pillar of stars
pulses ruby and violet.

Hour by hour,
we shed empty flasks,
outer layers.

We walk on.

In silence.

Wasteland

Sengai struggles.

By the third night,
he stumbles,
lies still on the ground.

The women march on
into the wasteland
of parched sand
and salt flats.

Sengai tells me to go.

But I stay.

Each word a labor,
he speaks:

> *Don't you see, Toshiro?*

> *You have to journey farther.*

> *You have to eclipse.*

> *The Synth must outshine.*

I give him the last flask.

I stare into the ice-blue light of the pillar,

watch the stars funnel down,
weigh his words.

Canabur shivers.

Salt crystals strew.

Dawn rises gold in the east.

I kneel down with Sengai,
speak kind and firm:

>   *If you are right,*
>   *then prove the Twins wrong.*
>
>   *Make their experiment fail.*
>
>   *I will carry a while.*
>
>   *You can eat, drink, and rest,*
>   *return twice as strong.*

Sengai breathes deep.

He sits up.

He drinks.

Sengai points to his feet,
says the blisters
are open and bleeding.

I untie his boots.

I peel off his socks.

The socks are heavy.

Soaked.

But not with red blood.

A viscous silver fluid
beads through the cloth.

I hide the socks,
study his feet grinded raw,
a synthetic mesh beneath skin.

Bronze

Sengai pushes hard
through the heat of the day.

He matches my pace,
stride for stride,
gritted teeth.

At sight of the women,
he leaves me behind.

Sengai smiles, laughs,
calls out to Sara.

They march together as the sun
descends from its midday peak.

Highlands break on the horizon.

Little domes,
brown and grey,
rise.

We kick pebbles,
clods.

The wasteland ends
in lunar hills.

Sara collapses against
the first boulder found.

Sengai falls, too,
by her side.

The guiding pillar of light
swallows the last star of the sky.

The pillar dissolves,
violet and blue.

Paranal stands,
the strongest of domes,
his wide shoulders
bright-lit by sun.

The old slump,
silent,
still,
breathe their last.

The sun,
so long cruel,
touches soft on their skin –
molten bronze glory.

Around us,
cloaks are lifted.

Hovers descend,
touch the ground.

Solemn and prayerful,
the Twins' servants move.

The servants lift Sara and Sengai,
take them away, lay them serene
in sarcophagi misting.

The cloaks return,
matching the dusk.

The hovers are gone
with a breeze.

Ichika walks for Paranal.

I walk, too.

Through night.

And day.

And night once more.

<u>Circling</u>

Ichika,
her mind and body
made for action,
marches straight to Paranal,
eager,
aggressive,
demanding of answers.

But I,
Toshiro,
wander long,
circle the mount,
remembering,
pondering,
humbled by questions.

Why was Sengai driven to failure?

Why was the creature destroyed by creators?

Why was his true nature hidden?

Why was he blind to deepest reflection?

His life was trapped circle.

Not linear climb.

He was the butterfly

of Chuang Tzu
dreaming of man.

A blue light
calls to me from
the mountain crest.

The hands of Ichika
moving in code:

Okonos.

Here.

Now.

Come.

I climb.

Every Skin

Brother Okono,
leans head and hip against
the observatory wall.

He faces the dawn,
his tired eyes mere slits of gold.

I stumble,
loose rocks.

Brother glances down,
pretends not to see me.

Ichika, at his side,
meets my eyes.

She shakes her head in warning.

She nods toward
the next observatory dome.

I traverse,
slow on the rock
of red dust and powder.

I climb steep Paranal,
sometimes crawling
hands and knees.

Above,
Sister Okono
leans to the wall
just as her brother.

She watches
the bright eastern sky
with eyes dark and heavy.

She dips seaweed in her tea,
licks her fingers.

Sister sees me.

She summons me higher.

I stand at her side.

Sister studies the eyes
of her servant and child.

She tosses tea dregs,
turns back to dawn.

Sister speaks with spent voice:

> *Toshiro, untiring,*
> *has traveled so far.*

> *Toshiro has questions.*

Why did the old have to die?

Why did his Mother and Father deceive?

She takes me by the hand.

She leads me
around the dome.

We stand together
at the wide gate entrance,
an open door to vaulted chamber.

Inside,
there are many.

Native Chileans
adjust the great telescope,
work with codes, charts, and screens.

Around the telescope,
I see the peoples of Earth,
every skin:
Euros. Russians.
Indians. Africans.
Islanders. Australians.
Americanos Norte and Sur.
Asians of the inland. Asians of the coast.

A handful stare,
hypnotic,

at a hologram sun,
coal-red churning,
gold-boiling loops of
convection and flare.

A few point
to midway stations and
mines of the Moon.

A few more
huddle around Mars,
point to colony specks,
touch the razor-thin air
of the surface.

All others watch the Earth slowly turn.

Planet Earth.

Her labored breath,
so hot and dry.

Her molten ranges
quivering red.

Her darkening seas
of dead-zone shadows.

Her spinning storms,
aurora green, white-slash lightning,
downpour torrents black.

Her ash-grey droughts and famines,
swelling tumors through the land.

Her fauna driven poleward,
bleeding sap-green waves.

Her flora like burnt umber,
withered around her waist.

Her wars like scarlet fires
windblown through straw fields.

The many peoples watch slow turn.

Some argue.

Some plead.

Some sleep on their feet.

A Chilean man,
broad of nose and cheek,
walks to the center of the crowd.

By a wave of his glove,
he evaporates
Earth,
Mars,
Moon,
and Sun.

By a second wave
appears a columned list
of times and speakers.

The Sister pulls me
from the vaulted chamber,
through the closing gate.

Debt and Duty

I watch the sunrise
with Sister Okono.

The sun shines
brilliant on the hills.

But it is
the turning Earth
that haunts and lingers.

I see Earth clear
in nightmare vision.

I see her many wounds and pains,
her wasting,
gasping,
burning,
tearing.

Pangs of birth or throes of death?

I cannot tell.

But over all the
vast and anguished Earth,
I am drawn to one thin thread.

I trace the line of seasteads.

Backward from Pacific coast.

Back from Darwin's island.

Into the heart of the sea.

Into the womb.

I wonder where.

I wonder why.

The Sister's voice once more pulls and wakes me:

> *The greatest of Earth*
> *fill that chamber, Toshiro,*
> *the greatest servants, greatest leaders,*
> *of Science, Art, Culture, Religion.*
>
> *We were summoned by the Chileans,*
> *drawn by hints of a message*
> *from the Stars.*
>
> *For three days now,*
> *the Chileans have listened to us speak;*
> *they have shared our grief and our dreams.*
>
> *But tomorrow,*
> *they will speak.*

I confess to the Sister my narrow vision,

my blindness to the whole.

Sister smiles:

So near, Toshiro, so near to the truth.

Sister prays with a hand of blessing:

May your eyes open
to the galaxies' full span.

By your weakness,
may you stretch and flex.

By your smallness,
may you join all life,
every interwoven sphere.

Sister kisses,
confesses her own:

Sengai was a Protal,
a Synth of the first generation.

Beneath their skin,
I buried a legion of errors.

The Protals paid dearly
for my young impatience,
my ignorance,
my pride.

I focused too much on the surface,
on blending and appearance.

I neglected the inner worlds,
avoided the harder work of
complex living systems.

I trusted organs grown by stem in isolation,
tissues unproven in long dynamic trial.

I built immune defenses
too rigidly aggressive,
too slow to adapt to
the changing world.

In the end,
I made chameleons.

Brother Okono
waits at the gate.

Sister raises a finger,
asking for time.

She raises her hair,
pins high the silver tangles.

She speaks to me
of the servant's duty,
of the species' debt
to Tree of Life:

The Protals must yield
to the Novals.

And the Novals will yield
to the newborn generation.

We are all swallowed
in the end, Toshiro.

We are all carried on
by the river.

Sister rejoins Brother.

Ichika waves.

Warnings

We enter the mantid drone.

We settle in the thorax,
an iridescent bulb
with fluid skin like sky.

Six legs lift from the ground,
thrust by cells of silver ember.

Paranal retreats.

The desert streaks
beneath our feet.

Ichika looks
and points behind:

Faraway Canabur vents
an orange-grey ashen column.

The wind-struck column plumes.

Dry lightning splinters white.

Our mantid skims low to the ground,
travels south and east.

The wide plume of Canabur narrows.

Then shrinks.

Then blends
in bank of clouds.

Our mantid smoothly weaves and bends
with the curving of the land.

The thorax fills with sounds
of the Paranal chamber…

A flurry of coughs through the crowd.

Light sandals
on hard metal stairs.

An introduction by Chilean.

The low, flat voice of
Brother Okono.

Brother argues for more farms and cities of the sea.

For the coming hours of debate,
he offers dual warning.

A warning
against inertia,
stalemate,
a rain of voices drowning ears.

And a counter-warning
against impatience,
stampede,
herds gathered under banner.

In a weak but passioned voice,
the Sister also warns.

The leaders have rushed to plan and build, she says,
without firm ground beneath their feet,
without unity of mind.

   Who is living? What is life?

   Can all be saved or only some?

   Should we cling fierce to equator
   or flee to the poles?

   Should we see Earth as last stand
   or launching pad to the stars?

Rocky hills pass below.

Lone guanacos
of shriveled flank
bite between stones.

Monks and Rangers

Razor

Higher and higher,
the mantid climbs.

We glide between the titan peaks.

We soar among the condors,
white sun bright upon dark wings.

We ride the gusts
of deep-carved valleys,
shadowed thick on floor.

Ichika changes in the light.

Her rounded flesh pulls down
in tightened skin and bone.

Her hair fades pale
with sunworn bleach.

Her lips crack dry,
seep blood through island scabs.

And deepcut wrinkles
slash her cheek.

She says:

> *We will be refugees of the water wars,*
> *farmers fleeing the sand-dry fields of Cuarto.*

We will join the dying
who burn with thirst,
who dream of surging falls
and swollen mountain lakes.

The mantid drops,
banks east.

Below -
a slender river.

Army camps ring the headwater pools.

Barracks line the merging highland streams.

By washed-out midland dams,
full battles rage:
artillery blasts cross-river,
rockets launch from cave to cave,
cliff walls split and crumble.

The river bends,
thins to lowland razor,
dies on bed of rocks,
straw yellow.

The mantid lands
on an abandoned ranch.

We run for the broken foothills.

Monje

We join a line of refugees,
campesinos without land,
scared families in flight.

We hug the hillsides,
cling to shadows;
we softly step
with fearful glances
ground to sky,
ahead,
behind,
between.

The campesino fathers
lead the way.

The fathers aim for the setting sun.

But the rock-channel maze
deflects straight course,
bends south,
juts north,
loops east.

At each disappointing turn,
the fathers argue with fierce whispers,
the mothers curse,
the children groan.

The heat of day
retreats from shade.

A darkened chill
crawls out from hollows.

Above,
a whirring,
whistling fan.

Green light descends from disc.

The campesinos hide.

In a cleft.

Every hand draws blade.

Ichika blocks the mouth.

Her palms
crackle blue,
electric;
white sparks ache
to bridge.

In a half-breath,
the hands of Ichika darken,
cross the air like serpent strike;
her long fingers wrap the throat.

But the stranger
raises bamboo staff,
in fluid motion
blocks,
checks,
pins to wall.

Blue fire burns in the eyes of Ichika.

I step between.

The children cry out:

    Monje! Monje!

They run to the monk,
hug his waist.

Machina

Marcos,
the barefoot monk.

With head shaved bare
to sun-pinked skin.

With black-waved beard
of jungle Che.

Marcos leads us
through the darkening hills
to a long-abandoned mine.

Trailing high,
his disc drone lights
the cavern mouth,
blocked by rotting timbers.

By levered staff,
the monk raises the timbers.

One by one,
we slide below.

When all are in,
lean Marcos slips through
slightest crack.

The disc lands
on highest timber,
perches stoic.

Its drone eye fills the cave
with warm faint yellow.

The campesinos circle Marcos.

The monk gives away capfuls of water
until his canteen runs dry;
for himself, he only wettens
dusty tongue.

I notice ink on his palms.

Tattoo stigmata.

Pierced wounds bleeding rainbow.

Marcos squeezes soy paste
into the hungry mouths around him.

He cuts the flattened tube open,
lets the children lick clean.

All shared,
the campesinos turn,
study Ichika.

They say, with fear:

> *Machina.*

The monk also studies Ichika.

And me.

I tell them part of truth:

> *We have come to serve*
> *from the Isle of Edo.*
>
> *Already we have helped*
> *the scientists at Cotopaxi,*
> *the Guarani of the jungle,*
> *the rescuers of Huaraz.*

Marcos,
weighing,
stares.

He glances to
the disc drone,
says he waits for orders.

In the cavern belly,
the refugees find
foil blankets,
straw mats,

socks and sandals.

They huddle,
sleep,
blades in hand.

The disc drone
flashes blue in signal.

Marcos hands us blankets.

Coyotes and Slavers

Deep in the night,
the drone flashes red.

We hurry from the cavern,
follow the amber-lit lanes of the disc.

The hills pass by -
a brown and grey blur
of split faces, cracked stone.

Another monk joins us,
warns of slavers north, coyotes south,
disappears.

A harder Marcos drives us;
he taps calves and heels,
prodding us forward by staff;
he scolds the sleepwalkers awake,
grunts at the laggers.

Ichika kneels by a stumbling boy,
lets him jump to her shoulders.

A girl climbs my back,
wraps my neck.

The way steepens.

Lanes narrow,
switch back and forth
in shear climb.

The refugees fight
weakened legs,
weary eyes,
burning thirst.

In the final push before dawn,
they join hands,
form a line.

They scale boulders together,
pull higher the faint,
lift the fallen from ground.

They cling to life,
stubborn and fierce.

The monk,
relieved,
smiles wide
as he pulls each climber
to safety in an aerie alcove.

He lets them sit,
rest,
breathe.

He pats shoulders,
points to a snowmelt pool
in the cove.

While the refugees drink,
Ichika looks down the great mount
we have climbed.

I follow her eyes.

Through the northern hills,
a wide front advances:

Slaver wagons.

Each flanked by gunners,
their cages near full.

I look to the south,
spot a refugee flock
in long valley.

Machete and pistol,
the coyote leads.

Bandits wait
at valley's end.

Sunset Glow

We climb little higher
through the day.

The altitude cripples.

Campesino hands puff red and white.

Feet swell against boots,
bruise, crack, bleed.

Lungs tighten, clench thin.

Heads dizzy and pound.

Marcos finds
a circle of stones:

Knee-high blocks
chiseled into the
teeth of puma and
condor wings.

He says a prayer,
starts a fire.

The monk stands
on the ledge like a falconer.

He whispers instruction,

commissions the drone.

The drone disappears in grey fog.

While the campesinos rest by the fire,
we speak with the monk.

Ichika asks of our plan for survival.

Marcos tells us
that soon he must leave
and return to the hills.

He reassures:

> *A ranger is coming to guide you.*
>
> *She is Dora Maria,*
> *the first of the mothers.*
>
> *And she is much greater than I.*

I ask of the journey to come.

He tells us instead
of the refugees' start.

Grinning humble, he says:

> *The Sisters of Clare*
> *are greater, too,*
> *braver and stronger.*

*The Sisters gather refugees
in the worst parts of worst cities.*

*They hide in church cellars,
dodge the slavers,
the drogas,
the tax-hunter sweeps.*

*They help forced mules
and conscripts escape.*

*Risking still more,
they move to the towns,
lead strikes at the sweatshops,
take those without hope
to the hills.*

*The Brothers of Francis
just climb for a day, maybe two.*

*We are too slow for the city,
too soft for the mountains.*

*We merely guide
from cave to cove.*

Out of the fog,
the disc drone appears,
drops a satchel.

Marcos unties, takes a leaf.

He presses the coca leaf
into his cheek,
works his tongue,
savors long.

The rest of the satchel he gives.

The refugees smile,
lay back, suck their leaves.

By the last light of day,
Ichika and I gather sticks,
pile up by the fire.

Marcos has left.

Alone on high mountain,
the refugees huddle.

Ichika says nothing,
pokes at the coals.

My eyes ride the ridgeline,
a swift-fading red.

I trace the galaxy's river:
slews of violet and gold,
hazel gems.

I wander the moon,
from crater to crater,
dust sea to dust sea.

A spark.

Above on the mountain.

I turn,
look high,
see the sunset glow of cigar.

I see boots dangling
over stone ledge,
a black beret under
pale moon.

Maria stares back,
narrow, curious eyes,
taps her ash.

Best of Men

Maria does not lead like Marcos.

Maria does not lead at all.

After each short break,
puffing lazy on cigar,
she points to distant landmarks:
a patch of brush,
a shadowed cave,
an odd-shaped boulder.

She shrugs away our questions,
tucks silver hair tangles under her beret,
waits for us to leave.

When I look back,
she is gone.

Ichika,
filling the void,
takes the front.

Though wanting to go fast,
Ichika sets a slow pace for
the mountain-sick.

I take up the rear,
moving slow,
scanning behind,

up and down both valley flanks.

But I never catch sight of
the ranger moving.

She is always ahead, far ahead,
sitting on the ridgeline,
boots over ledge.

Puffing slow,
she watches us pass;
her dark eyes lock onto
the climbers struggling most;
she sees every grimace,
every stumble, every limp.

By midday,
one family is finished:
the father's feet raw and bleeding,
the son blinded by cruel headache,
the mother drifting and confused.

Maria sits them down by a basin pool.

She gives them long drinks from her canteen,
then coca leaves, then sun-bleached roots.

Maria kneels between
the father and son,
rubs their shoulders.

She says that lowest Patagonia
needs good farmers, strong farmers,
the best of men.

She asks them humbly
for their help.

The son looks to his father.

The father nods,
a light returned to his eyes.

The mother asks
how they will travel
to distant Patagonia.

Maria tells them to rest at the pool,
to wait for help from the sky.

Before the march continues,
Maria pulls me aside.

Dark eyes peering deep,
she says:

> *Machina,*
> *switch with your sister.*

> *Take the lead.*

> *You will follow the*

bones of dead glacier.

Machina,
stop looking for me
in the valley.

Drive the refugees hard.

I set strong pace.

Trust

The glacier,
once towering and wide,
now survives only in ponds of mud,
shallow and scattered.

But the dying river
had ravaged the ground
in its long retreat.

Grinding ice had split
and ripped the mountain stone
like a tiger's claw through silk.

Bleeding melt streams
had gouged fresh channels,
carved sharp spurs over land,
eaten bedrock jagged.

And ice-chewed till had
coughed out long mounds,
trails of sand and gravel.

I lead through the
melt stream channels,
over the dry beds
and thick pebbled sheets.

When the channels
fork, rise, end,

I long-step
cobble to cobble.

When blocked by crevasse,
I run the chasm's length
and search for narrow crossing.

The refugees fight for breath,
struggle on.

They fall behind.

Farther and farther.

Ichika, passing,
strides up the line,
works her way from rear to front.

She scans the high walls
of the valley,
calls out for Maria.

Unanswered,
she tells me to stop:

   Shadows are long, Toshiro.

   The families drift.

   A cold night is coming.

I look down the dead river,
see no end.

Mist tails rise from the chasms.

A high fog settles.

Behind,
a refugee father
shouts out.

He calls all together,
orders long rest.

Ichika turns back.

I push ahead,
coursing dry beds,
leaping chasms.

A short whistle.

Maria.

Close by.

She speaks through the mist:

One machina trusts.

One rebels.

Sheaves

The morning sun
reaches timid into the cave.

An orange haze glows
in highest vault.

Red beams widen, slant,
brighten yellow on the wall.

Maria sits in the cavern mouth.

Her grey hair shines pale gold
in the strengthening light.

Hard eyes to horizon,
her fingers turn an unlit stub.

The families stir
in the cavern heart.

They break away from
their warming huddles.

They roll up their blankets,
rub stiff necks, stretch sore legs.

But no one leaves the cave.

All eyes stare down

at the cavern floor.

The ranger's bag lies flat,
turned inside-out,
picked completely bare
save a line of crumbs
and a single stem.

Maria rises,
tosses her stub.

Today,
Maria leads.

She leads quickly.

Away from the high glacier bed.

Through a stone pass
slender and shadowed.

Down into the keel of a steep ravine.

Maria descends
without a backward glance.

Without rest,
she pushes on.

From pass to pass.

Through forests of crag.

Through canyons gusty and misted.

And trickling arroyos clear.

Ichika,
light foot,
stays the closest,
though sometimes losing sight.

I trail back,
midway to the refugees,
bridging the wide and dangerous gap.

Behind,
I hear harsh whispers,
blame thrown back and forth.

Late-day clouds thicken grey,
threaten rain.

Ichika,
far ahead,
out of view,
leaves guiding strips
of red cloth in the brush.

Young Pedro runs to me
with sister, Jasmine.

Still strong,
they say to catch up to Ichika:

We will fill the gap.

I hurry on.

A light rain falls.

Around a wide butte,
I find four strips.

The clouds turn black,
downpour swift.

Then,
just as sudden,
scatter.

I face a cliff wall.

Ichika and Maria
stand dry beneath an
outcrop slab.

Roots,
sun-bleached honey and saffron,
climb from a dark-soiled garden.

The roots branch,
twine,

braid,
across the
west-facing wall.

Fan-shaped sheaves of the roots,
freshly cut,
lie atop boulders.

Jasmine calls back to Pedro.

Pedro calls back to his father.

Soon,
all the refugees gather.

They face Maria over the
rich-harvest boulders.

Confessions pour out.

The guilty step forward.

Maria forgives
with sad eyes,
nodding slow.

She ladens the guilty
with generous sheaves.

She tells them the way
to the first lowland village.

Maria winces as the
innocent join the guilty in march -
exile shared to keep families together.

She calls out,
tells them to find
the casita ringed by white roses,
tended by blind Sister Ana.

Of all the refugees,
only the family of Jasmine and Pedro
remains in the highlands.

Teachers

Maria changes after
the sifting at the cliff.

A weight has been lifted from her,
a burden shed,
a freedom gained.

Maria warms,
even to Machinas.

She leads us back
into the mountains.

She shows us secret paths,
hidden coves,
nestled dens.

She teaches us how to read the
sudden shifting moods of the clouds,
their subtle whites and greys,
the signs before the storm.

She opens our eyes
to ancient guides and markers:
shrines, tombs, symbols carved in stone.

She shares the names of the mountains,
tells stories of their birth and youth,
describes their many faces.

In garden patches under sun,
she shows us strangest fare:

New hybrid plants of
interwoven seeds.

Experiments of the Chileans.

Gifts for the rangers.

Pedro picks thorns,
licks a milk-cream honey
bleeding from the branch.

Jasmine slices open stem spears,
finger-scoops a meaty paste.

Their parents try
long cinnamon beans,
saliva-melted pods and husks,
sweet kernel seeds of blue stout fern,
a purple moss that crackles on the tongue.

Day by day,
we march and climb.

We end each day at water.

Falls towering and misted.

Lagoons of crystal emerald.

Lakes with geese and gulls.

We talk
beneath the starry river
deep into the night.

Jasmine rests at Maria's side,
begs stories of the rangers.

Maria tells of terror in the city.

The warlords' clash.

Her three sons lost in a year.

Her husband hung from bridge.

She had fled to the mountains.

Maria, too,
had been a refugee,
weak from hunger,
lost,
afraid.

But the indio had found her;
the healer had saved.

Antonio,
kind Antonio,
had guided her safely

through the hills of killer and thief.

Antonio,
wise Antonio,
had taught her secret paths,
the whites and greys of the clouds,
the sacred mountain names.

Brief Bend

Maria lets young Pedro lead.

His path bends east
to lowland hills.

We enter a greenless canyon.

With dusty walls of
red and amber.

With crumbling mesas
long and grey.

We walk the
pebble-sand bed
of a dry parched stream.

The stagnant air
hangs heavy with smoke.

Eyes redden and water.

Bandanas cover mouths
coughing from the soot.

With a short whistle,
Maria calls young Pedro back,
retakes the lead.

Eyes high and low,
she breaks away from
the exposed stream.

We follow her close
through the smoky haze.

We cling
to the mesa walls.

We dash
from mount to mount.

At the canyon's end,
Maria allows no rest.

She leads us west
to higher hills.

Sweet winds stir.

We climb from
the thick-banked smoke
into purer airs.

Bandanas are lowered
to cough and to spit.

Maria stops at the
first mountain pass.

Head hung low,
Pedro weathers rebuke
from mother,
father.

But Maria pats the boy's shoulder,
shrugs away error.

She pulls
spikes and ropes
from her pack.

She says with a grin:

> *Pedro's bold leading*
> *has given us chance to*
> *learn a new skill.*
>
> *Tomorrow,*
> *we climb*
> *wild as goats.*

Fingers and Thumb

Maria tests us through the day.

The ranger ropes my waist,
makes me lead and anchor.

We work through crags
by the morning sun.

We hop low pillars.

We weave our way
through a stairstep maze.

From crags' end,
we round the flank of Pulgar,
forced slow around the mountain's spurs.

We trace the
blade of a narrow ridgeline,
higher,
higher.

White mists
sweep across our feet,
hide our boots.

The farmers gasp
with each new gust.

We climb.

We climb.

We step out suddenly
on a high plateau.

Maria whistles
me to stop,
allows long drink.

Looking back,
Pulgar seems so small.

Looking up,
his brothers tower high.

Maria, sharing kernels, says:

> *We have only climbed*
> *the short thumb,*
> *my friends.*
>
> *Now,*
> *tall fingers*
> *come.*

Maria unties,
takes the lead.

The ranger stares long

up the veins of the next mountain.

She chooses her gully,
narrow, unbroken.

She climbs,
teaching young Jasmine the spikes.

I take up the rear,
try to talk with Ichika.

But Ichika says little,
won't meet my eyes.

Through the hard day,
I watch her.

Her movements are wrong.

Her fingers twitch.

Her arm hangs limp.

Her feet miss their mark,
paw through the air,
desperate for ground.

<u>Dreams</u>

Seven mounts in seven days.

The ranger's goal is set.

And reached.

Down final gully,
no one speaks.

We untie ropes.

We savor silence.

The wind smells rich and green.

A valley sprawls below.

A forest thickens.

Dark lenga beech slant and crook.

Bare-trunked araucaria towers
burst wide at their crown.

Triumphant,
we descend.

Entering the woods,
we catch glimpses of the pudu deer,

kicking mud from tiny hooves,
and flashes of wing,
bird breasts yellow, white, and green.

We stop and camp in an open glade,
gather wood for fire.

We eat,
drink,
rest.

Near dusk,
Maria rises by the fire,
her face aglow,
eyes bright with pride.

She speaks to the family:

> *By our great journey*
> *you have grown.*
>
> *You are now friends to me.*
>
> *And all my friends are yours.*
>
> *Our mestizo brothers and sisters*
> *work farms and orchards*
> *by the lakes of Patagonia.*
>
> *Our indios herd sheep and llamas*
> *in the deep south hills.*

Our strong friends of Indonesia,
forced from homes by swollen sea,
now fish and crab our western coast.

Our great Indian family works the fjords,
building turbines, pumps, and stations,
tapping power of the wave.

All these would welcome you.

And Maria speaks to us, Machinas:

You, too, have learned and grown.

You, too, are precious friends.

But I do not offer you an open choice.

In the deepest mountains,
you must find Antonio.

Antonio,
kind Antonio,
wise Antonio,
will heal Ichika's sickness.

Beside the fire,
the family talks
deep into the night.

After all choices have been weighed,

the family settles on the new life
nearest to the old:
farming by the lakes.

The father dreams of
electric harvesters and plows.

The mother dreams of
potato stew, tomatoes dripping juice,
twilight walks without gunfire.

Pedro dreams of
science books, new boots,
soccer on grass fields.

But Jasmine shares no dream.

She sneaks away,
whispers with Maria.

And I speak with Ichika.

I tell her that we can summon a drone.

She can return to the Twins,
be healed by the Sister's hand.

Ichika laughs,
calls me fool,
says all was set at birth.

Jasmine stands
above her family's huddle.

She pleads with her father,
says that she was not born to live
the farmer's life of dirt and weeds.

She begs her mother for a chance
to travel the mountains free –
a ranger.

Jasmine trembles
through her hands.

The fire crackles.

Her mother reaches,
pulls her down into the
warming huddle.

Her father turns away,
says she is free,
now and forever.

Pedro touches,
also turns.

Antonio

El Cabro

Day by day,
Ichika struggles.

She tells me that her vision,
once sharper than a hawk,
now fails by
haze-smeared trailers,
sudden flashes of darkness,
encroaching pools of shadow.

Her ankles twist among the stones.

Her knees sometimes lock,
sometimes give.

She walks without confidence.

She pauses after each step,
braces, tense,
for fall or stumble.

She takes up one staff,
then another,
gripping tight with
shaking fingers.

But Ichika refuses
my helping hand.

She tells me that
mine is the weaker vision:

*How can the Twins
craft the next generation
without knowing our flaws?*

*Every weakness revealed in me
will lift my children higher.*

She pulls me nearer:

*We must live as
meteors bound for land,
our bright fire streaking,
burning through skin after skin.*

When we reach El Cabro,
the two-horned mountain,
Ichika sits down on a boulder.

She smiles,
breathes deep.

Remembering the words of Maria,
we wait for a rising of wind,
a scattering of clouds.

When the sun breaks through,
the sheer northern horn beams
a brilliant gold.

The gold reflected
lights a slender trail
through the lesser mounts.

I point to the trail.

Ichika squints,
nods without seeing.

El Potro

The trail passes
a pen
edged by wood stakes.

Inside,
three sheep and a pig
nibble brush stalks.

Above,
a young shepherd
plays a bone flute in
the crook of a tree.

He pauses when he sees us.

He nods at my wave,
returns to his song.

The trail climbs on
to a higher plateau.

The trail weaves
through thickening trees.

The ear of Ichika,
still sharp,
tilts to hear.

She raises a finger,

points far.

I catch a glimpse through the trees:
a horse packing branches
tied by a rope.

The trail bends
around boulders.

The plateau rises,
steepens again.

Ichika rests for a moment.

Eyes closed,
mouth open,
she basks in the sun.

The forest thins.

Green brush yellows.

The tree trunks narrow
to sapling poles.

The trail turns toward
a flat-topped butte.

Then the trail peaks.

And descends.

We hear the crash of water,
see the falls white and blue.

A stream rushes down from the falls.

Our trail veers,
joins the stream.

The stream quiets,
slows,
clears,
crawls down to a village:

Ten huts in a ring.

Built of mud, grass, and stone.

A woman in beige shawl
lowers bundles from the horse,
feeds branches to the fire.

She gives a loud-whistled summons.

The villagers pour out of the huts.

Pots are boiled over the fire,
potatoes thrown in.

Wood pipes are blown,
a guitar of four strings is played.

Corn beer is scooped into clay bowls,
passed hand to hand.

The villagers talk,
laugh,
sing,
dance.

We approach the villagers' fire.

We try to tell them of our friend, Maria,
and our search for the healer, Antonio.

The woman in beige shawl
shakes her head, stops our story.

She brings us hot soup and warm beer.

With a broken-toothed smile, she says:

> *Tomorrow, tomorrow,*
> *tell us tomorrow.*

> *Today, we celebrate*
> *a blessed new birth.*

The villagers turn away from us.

They walk to the open field, shout:

> *Potro! El potro!*

They cheer for a
foal kicking long legs,
bucking and leaping.

Obsidian

The villagers wake to damp fog.

They grab buckets,
hurry up the hill,
gather potatoes
drying in the grass.

The villagers run back,
just beating the rain.

We are welcomed inside a smoky hut.

Alpaca skins hang from pole rafters.

A boy feeds the fire dried dung.

Everyone stares at us
over bowls of hot broth.

Their eyes,
morning sober,
notice the nose of Ichika
hollowed on one side,
her patches of skin
worn down to mesh.

We tell them our story.

They sip and they nod.

They tell us that Antonio is not well.

His mother and father have died.

His whole village was destroyed
by an earthquake and flood.

When we ask where to find him,
a young man leads us from the hut.

Young David takes us up the stream,
past the blue-white falls roaring loud,
up the butte's side by a long slanted cleft.

On the top of the butte,
David points to a mountain chain
far to the south.

One mount in the chain
glows bright by red seeping ring.

Another vents steam.

Another black ash.

The eyes of David
– deep obsidian –
show sadness and fear.

He says that Antonio has gone
to face the spirits of the mountains,

the gods of fire and quake.

He says that he has lost
his father and teacher.

Ichika says that she is dying.

She goes to face the same gods.

We ask him to join us
as friend.

Pachamama

David makes many offerings
on the long journey.

At outcrop shrines,
he leaves carnations red and white,
feathers of the condor,
images of saints.

At crystal springs,
he burns the seeds
of bean and tree.

He enters caverns,
prays at altars;
he sprinkles
corn and coca leaves,
pours wine, and
lights the fire.

Outside,
he shares with us
the teachings of Antonio:

The cave is womb,
the altar round like
Sun and Earth.

We give in thanks
for all we have received

from Pachamama.

*The fire transforms our offering
into Spirit and Light.*

Life is renewed.

Balance restored.

Ichika dreams along our journey.

She sees a future land of sun and ice
and quiet, golden rivers.

The mountains thaw,
bleed life into the soil.

Her sons plant trees
and sleep in starry fields.

Her daughters mix with dolphins,
swim free among the melting bergs.

But I have no dreams
in the night.

I cannot rest.

I move my fingers,
always numb,
clenching and unclenching.

I feel the mesh outline
under my windworn cheek,
touch the first thread
breaking through skin.

I rub my rock-grinded knees,
the knees that tremble when I stand
and groan with each step.

Penitentes

David,
trying for shortcut,
leads us straight up a hill of loose rock.

Our feet sink deep in the gravel.

With each step gained,
we slide downhill.

Leaning low,
we claw with our hands
through the stones,
crawl like lizards in mudslide.

David stops,
midhill,
coughing hoarse,
blinded by dust and sweat
in his eyes.

He lays on his back,
spits to the side.

To Ichika, he asks:

   Why? Why do you seek him?

Ichika lays down beside,
stares up at the sky,

answers:

> *Because of the Monks of Saint Francis*
> *and the Sisters of Clare.*

> *Because of Maria, the mother and ranger.*

> *Because I want more time.*

We retreat from the hill,
return to the trail.

The trail threads the low ground
between mounting hills.

We climb,
bend to bend,
turn to turn.

David pauses to scan a canyon below.

He points to the cliff with a smile.

I see two perches
marked with white droppings.

And between the perches -
a ledge, a nest of dry branches.

A fledgling condor,
thick with grey down,

stands at the edge.

The fledgling,
shaking,
watches the circling
of mother and father,
plunges to join.

David climbs on, says:

> *Soon, we will face our own edge.*

The trail leads on.

The air thins and thins.

The sun falls from zenith.

On the final slope before summit,
a strange sight appears.

A field of white spires
like monk hoods.

Thin-bladed ice.

Curving toward sun.

David names the kneeling throng:

> *Penitentes.*

Lovers of Inti,
the Sun.

We slip through the spires,
pass through long shadows.

Ichika moves slow,
touching the white ice,
feeling each curve.

At the summit,
we gaze across a deep valley.

The mountain chain
of fire and quake is no longer far.

The lava-ringed mount stands near.

Orange rivulets run from the ring,
darken red as they fall, crust over brown,
black by the foot.

Heat from the mount boils the air,
strips every mist, scatters the clouds.

We camp for the night.

Sleepless,
we stare.

Tribes

David and Ichika
talk through the night.

Their eyes glow red
with the mountain's fire.

Ichika asks:

> *Do you see me*
> *as living creature*
> *or lifeless tool?*

David, after long thought, answers:

> *You are not lifeless.*

> *The machina*
> *moves and acts*
> *like any human.*

> *You change and learn.*

> *You age and fade.*

> *You live, like all,*
> *by the gift of time.*

Ichika asks if he feels
hope or despair for the future.

David tells of a meeting
three years ago on this same summit,
when the fiery range had just begun
to smoke and shiver.

The people of many mountain tribes and villages
had gathered to talk of the future.

Dark fears were shared:
the floods of melting glaciers,
a fungus ruining soil,
the dying trees,
withered grasslands,
shrinking herds.

Then brightest hopes:

Some dreamed
of the Incan Sixth Age,
the ancestors' return
by bridge of snake and dragon.

Some trusted
in the ageless power
of Pachamama,
believing that the Earth
would heal herself.

Others hoped that
the good mountain spirits
would overthrow the cruel.

All through the day,
Antonio listened.

At night,
he finally spoke:

    These are the pains of birth.

    A new world breaks from womb.

Prayers

There is no well-traveled trail
to the vulcan range.

We follow
a single set of tracks
through the valley, ·
light footprints stamped
in the grey-brown dust,
pebbles pressed in mud.

The tracks work toward the fiery range
but widely drift the valley floor,
veering wall to wall
like drunken steps.

On our third day in the valley,
the strides of Antonio lengthen;
his veering ends;
his tracks head straight
for the red-ringed mountain.

Straight,
we push into the searing heat,
into the haze of smoke and sulfur.

David struggles,
coughing,
sweating.

The ground begins to climb.

The air around us warps
like waves of violent sea.

Red streams
creep down the rising slope.

We have lost the tracks.

We circle back.

We find the last approaching steps.

Then knee-prints in the dirt.

Like his teacher,
David kneels and prays.

Dripping steady sweat,
he pleads for the Mountains' peace
and for Machina's healing.

Ichika kneels beside.

To the sky,
she raises hands,
weathered, peeling.

She prays
for the Humans' place

in the new world breaking forth.

I find new tracks of Antonio,
leading away from the mountain,
deeper into range.

Night March

We walk through the night
under cloudless sky.

The full moon shines
by white-pore craters
and blue-desert seas.

The milky river of stars
flows down marine,
floods the mountains with
violet and gold.

David, exhausted,
enters a higher state.

Of clarity.

And pain.

David speaks of the quake
in Antonio's village…

The earth torn
by rifts as wide as a hut.

The bodies lifted
from chasms by horses and ropes.

Antonio's father,

crushed between boulders,
buried too deep to raise.

He speaks of the flood
soon after the quake…

The battered survivors
struck by new terror.

The bodies swept, spun, tossed.

Antonio's mother,
wrapped in tangles of weeds,
found miles from home,
bloated in gully.

The tracks
enter a canyon
skirting the range.

A tremor,
slow-grinding,
sends cracks
through the walls.

Flakes of cinder and ash
float down like fresh snow.

The canyon forks
in three veins.

Our vein
- the southern -
breaks straight for
the heart of the range.

We climb
through rough crags.

We follow the tracks
over steep rising slopes.

At sunrise,
we reach a higher plateau.

Two mountains loom.

Left,
a high-coned mount
spews out clouds of white ash.

Right,
a great pyramid of stone
shakes through its base,
looses boulders.

David stops at a stream.

He washes soot from his face,
dunks his head.

Together,

we wait for
the lagging Ichika.

I ask him to rest,
to sleep for an hour.

Eyes glazed,
he packs leaves in his cheek,
shakes his head,
asks me:

Machina, what ground is safe?

Secret

We climb on.

We thread the tracks
between the two mountains,
ignoring all tremors,
brushing ash from our eyes.

David shares Antonio's secret
of the endless march:

> *Forget the long journey behind.*

> *Deny all the pain yet ahead.*

> *Narrow your world*
> *to the thin-slivered present.*

> *Ride its blade.*

> *Think of only next step.*

We step.

Step.

Step.

The two mountains pass.

A third approaches.

We keep our eyes low.

The tracks blur into shadow.

A hard rain falls at twilight,
washes the tracks.

Under a lone araucaria,
we shelter and
wait.

<u>Shards</u>

We wait.

And wait.

But the rain does not stop.

A shroud
of blue and grey clouds
wraps the mountain before us.

The great mountain quakes.

Fissures gash through its flanks,
throbbing red molten stone.

Through the fissures
launch geysers of smoke;
steam hisses on mixing
with the cold wind of night.

Bursts of silver-veined lightning
rip through the shroud;
the fleeing clouds
flash purple,
then white.

Ichika, sitting,
leans into the tree.

She closes her eyes,
covers her ears from
the thunder and quake.

David lays his cloak
across her shoulders.

He looks to the mountain,
speaks to me:

>   *Antonio is there.*

>   *Against him,*
>   *the spirits pour out*
>   *their rage.*

We leave Ichika.

We head up the mountain
by a narrow ravine.

We slip and stumble
through the rain-slick rocks.

After cloudbursts,
we crawl into the sudden flash streams,
brace against torrents.

David, cursing,
pulls me from the ravine.

We hide in a cleft.

David,
feeling full danger,
trapped by flood
in a tomb of rock,
says:

    This is the terror they knew.

Powerless, helpless,
we wait out the rain.

In the night's waning hours,
we move.

We straddle the trickling stream.

We climb the ravine,
stepping slow,
testing each hold.

David finds a break in the wall.

He leads through a passage to ridgeline.

He steps onto a ledge.

He sees his teacher below.

Antonio

stands alone
in a field of jagged rock.

Antonio stares, rapt,
into pools of still rain:

Mirrors of crystal reflecting bright lightning.

Shards alive with the glow of the stars.

Healing

Together,
we flee from the range.

Antonio leads
to an underground spring.

We strip and wash
in the steam-misted ponds.

David dresses,
dozes against me.

Antonio prays for Ichika.

The healer opens
his brown woolen bag,
lays out crystals and stones.

He handcups water
onto red-blistered scoria.

He touches her forehead
with snowflake obsidian.

To her heart,
he holds obelisk jade.

He lays in her palms
twin teardrops of lapis lazuli.

Antonio reaches deeper into his bag.

He mixes herbal powders
in tree saps and bronze-honeyed pitch.

He covers the hollow of her nose.

He coats each skinless patch.

Ichika asks what he saw on the mountain.

Antonio answers:

I saw the mirrored sky shattered.

And the high stars brought low.

I saw the first waters of life
sparked by Creator.

I saw power unbounded
and undying light.

I saw the end through beginning.

And beginning through end.

<u>Blind</u>

Antonio and David
return
to the north.

We travel south,
ever south,
over dry glacier beds,
down steep mountain passes,
through canyons of the condor
and valleys of the fox.

We reach
the Andes' low tail
by new moon.

Ichika is blind.

Silver bleeds freely
from her hands, brow, and feet.

Wet cheekbones of graphene
break through.

I summon the drone.

<u>Statue</u>

A gust sweeps the hilltop.

An osprey hover uncloaks.

From beneath wings' crook,
the Twins appear.

Sister Okono walks,
kneels by Ichika.

Sister touches
the torn skin of her face,
her deep nasal cavern exposed,
her lidless and unseeing eyes.

Blind Ichika
knows who touches,
turns her head,
asks forgiveness:

> *I came so far.*

> *I came so close
> but could not finish.*

Gripping hand, Sister blesses:

> *You will rest now,
> enshrined.*

You will dream,
free of pain.

You will wait
in sweet peace
for your children.

Brother Okono
lifts and cradles Ichika,
takes her away:

We are proud,
my daughter,
so proud.

Sister turns to me:

And you, Toshiro?

Are you finished?

Are you eager to sleep?

I look at my palms,
worn down to mesh.

I think
of my feet
grinded raw,
my knees
groaning and torn,

the weary list of my spine.

And I see Ichika laid in her tomb,
the frozen mists sealing,
turning to statue.

I answer Sister:

   No.

   I still burn.

Sister tells me to wait at the sea.

Southern End

<u>The Eel</u>

A mammoth eel
writhes backward to shore,
banks on the sand.

Gills angle out -
an opening door.

I slip inside.

The great eel
writhes forward,
plunges below.

Through its scales,
the emerald-blue sea
shimmers clear.

Fluid light sways.

Wind ripples stir.

Waves crash and swell.

Through the bends of the eel,
I see many riders,
many skins light and dark.

I recognize faces
from the meeting at Paranal,

the gathering of leaders
in the telescope chamber.

An Indian man takes my hand,
guides me to the head of the eel.

We sit down together,
facing the sea.

His cheek shines bronze
in the sea light,
his dark beard climbs to
round the bone.

His name is Manar, he says.

Manar sees
my lobeless ears,
my windtorn brow,
my shredded hands.

He asks my generation,
Protal or Noval?

I tell him the Protals are dead.

And the Novals are dying.

The great eel parts
a school of mackerel;
one cloud becomes three.

The eel follows the coast.

I ask our destination.

Manar says:

> *First,*
> *Corcovado,*
> *the crowded gulf.*
>
> *Then,*
> *the fjords*
> *of deep south.*
>
> *My friend,*
> *the gulf will sadden you,*
> *sicken and tear.*
>
> *But in the fjords you will see*
> *Siddhartha's pride.*

Kingdoms

The eyes of the eel
brighten with sunfall –
twin golden moons of the deep.

We talk through the night.

I tell Manar of my long mountain journey.

He tells me of the eel, his creation:

Her scales, by brace and flex,
capture every pitch and roll of the sea,
each turned to power.

She can stretch herself vertical
and store great reserves by
the difference in heat
head to tail.

He calls the past
a long reign of fools,
ages wasteful and dark,
fueled by fire.

He dreams of the dawning new world.

He praises the new science
drawing from bottomless well,
tapping the tireless wind,

yoking the power of
Sun, Moon, and Sea.

Below,
kingdoms pass.

The eyes of the eel
light forests and gardens.

Beds of seagrass
sway with the tide.

Kelp trees climb high;
their wide fronds float
like wind-lifted flags.

Coral sprawls
in a rainbow of color
and wide-varied shapes:
spiked staghorn pink and blue,
broad orange plates like pads of the lotus,
spiraling ribbon leaf, outpouring petals.

The eyes of the eel
dim with sunrise.

The forests shrink and thin.

The bright-colored gardens
yield to grey sand.

Manar warns that
the gulf is near.

Red Tide

Manar dozes against Chasca.

Chasca,
wife and pilot,
guides the great eel
by an amethyst spall in her lap.

Her black-latticed gloves
throb with strange light,
rays short-lived and probing,
draining of color.

The bright amethyst pales
at her touch;
the spall softens
like wax near to flame.

Chasca works undulations through the eel,
rhythmic waves through her palms;
she chooses eel's course
by the tips of her fingers.

A merchant carrier passes above us.

By the tilt of her hands,
the eel dives lower,
avoiding the carrier's wake.

Manar sits up.

He summons a holo,
points nearer to shore.

The hands of Chasca lean left.

The eel enters waters
the color of blood.

We bend right,
parallel to shore.

We ride the edge
of murky red clouds.

A webbed haze
shines through the billows:
a silver pall of dead fish.

Manar tells me it is
an algae bloom, a toxic plague,
a tide striking wider, crueler each year.

Chasca,
born on Chiloé,
speaks, too:

>   *The shore is even worse
>   than the sea.*
>
>   *The deep-piled dead
>   rot into marsh.*

A silver bog
spans full horizon.

And the smell,
never forgotten,
drifts far over land.

The Gulf

We enter the gulf.

Its waters are tainted
by rainbows of leaked fuel,
dark swaths of oil,
inky black grease.

We slip below
a chaos of traffic:
tankers, cruisers,
trawlers, reefers.

We pass slow-bobbing
isles of debris:
plastic bergs white, blue, and green,
shredded nets, rusted barrels,
sacks of garbage half-torn.

We skirt the murk-shadowed fish farms,
watch salmon break from rotting cages.

Dead-zone
to dead-zone,
we ride.

In the first port,
we surface a moment.

We watch pipes' unbroken stream

of runoff dregs, sewage sludge,
chemical slurry.

Manar points to sea:

   Enough.

Pod

We ride
through the night
in deep sea.

Chasca sleeps, reclined,
hands still swaying.

Manar trusts the eel
to AI pilot.

He joins a circle
of the sleepless
in debate:

A physicist questions
the Chilean decoding.

A mathematician wants access
to the raw message data.

Several others lobby
for a lift of the ban
on AI merging.

One argues loudly
for the freeing of Dio.

Many more argue against.

Manar says he trusts the Chileans,
urges patience.

Manar leaves the circle,
returns to eel's head.

Drained,
he stares into the
smooth flowing sea
of the holo.

The eel,
translucent green,
glides on and on.

Around,
the sea sleeps barren,
save a few preying fish -
specks of grey.

Manar asks me
if the Twins shared
the message from the stars.

I shake my head.

He nods, considers,
decides against sharing.

He asks if I love life,
fear death.

I watch the eel,
no more than worm,
glide through the unbounded sea.

I answer:

> *I understand now*
> *the work of the Sister,*
> *the strains that she buried*
> *deep under skin.*
>
> *I was given*
> *a poet's eye,*
> *a servant's humility,*
> *a zealot's blind faith.*
>
> *I was born to follow.*
>
> *Not lead.*
>
> *I am only a witness,*
> *my friend.*
>
> *Only a plodder.*

He asks, again,
of fear and death.

I answer with the questions
long haunting,
eluding:

Who can bend time?

Who can hold back the river?

Who can draw life from the void?

Behind the eel,
a pod approaches.

Dolphins,
white bellies,
black backs.

Manar sits up.

He smiles,
unburdened.

The sea flashes dark
as each dolphin races
by the eel's beaming eyes.

The dolphins slow,
wander wide,
let us pass.

The eel, unphased,
moves on through the deep.

The dolphins race by once more,
slapping tails to our scales,

clicking tongues.

I ask Manar
if the dolphins know that
the eel is machine.

Manar grins:

Of course.

Even God can't fool
a dolphin.

Mother and Calf

Chasca pilots again in the morning;
the amethyst melts into hand.

She trails two whales:
a mother and calf.

She creeps nearer and nearer,
closer to the surface,
closer to tail.

Manar whistles, excited,
to the riders behind us.

The leaders crowd close for a view.

We watch the whale flukes
rise in languid arches,
whip-strike down
with obscene power;
our great eel trembles in the wake.

Chasca creeps nearer.

We see frost-white splotches
on the whales' dark bellies.

Chasca creeps nearer.

Under their jaws,

we see salt-white calluses,
broken shells in pale cement.

The calf breaches,
crashes down.

The mother, protective,
dives toward us,
pursues.

Chasca, smiling,
veers the eel and plunges deep.

The mother whale rejoins her calf.

The leaders breathe.

Fjords

Chasca enters the fjords
through a wide-channeled gateway.

The eel rides the surface,
rearing to breach, plunging beneath,
revealing the worlds high and low.

Manar beams
at the homecoming.

He serves as narrating guide.

He points out
otters deep-diving for crab;
islet sea lions basking in the sun;
cormorant colonies loud on white spits;
rockhopper penguins
jumping from cliffs and
launching up ledges.

Chasca slows in a bay
beneath glacier.

The eel dodges
small floating bergs,
drifting floes.

We surface
in an open patch
near to the glacier.

We gaze up
at the ice wall
filling our sky.

Manar,
nervous,
nudges his wife,
speaks to me:

>   *Last year
>   a fortress of calved ice
>   broke free, rolled the eel.*

Chasca grins, turns the eel
from the wall:

>   *The ice was more
>   splinter than fortress.*

Manar mumbles
about two-week repair.

Back in the channel,
we return to full speed.

Steep islands pass by,
ringed with white fog,
thick with tussock and beech.

Manar points
to birds on the islands,
names their species in Latin.

Chasca frowns,
corrects to their older
indigena name.

We see fewer birds
as day fades toward night.

A front of dark storm clouds
sweeps in from the east.

Swift gales rough the seas,
severs waves white.

Chasca tilts her hands.

The eel plunges deep.

Lightning warps strange
through the waters above.

We wait out the storm.

Turbines

As suddenly as it came,
the storm calms.

The amethyst glows again
under Chasca's hands.

The eel cruises forward,
eases up from the depths.

Manar plots a course on the holo.

From the streak of his finger,
a tunnel of throbbing gold light
wraps the eel.

The tunnel starts in wide circle,
curves through long canyon,
narrows to a wire in a faraway strait.

Chasca,
annoyed by the
bright guiding tunnel,
orders it dimmer,
brightens the eyes of the eel.

The hands of Chasca work.

The eel writhes
smooth,
swift.

The distant strait nears.

Manar tells me of
the first colony in the bay,
led by his mother and father.

He tells me how the colony
was many times saved by aid
from the Okono Twins,
the Australians,
and the Fuegans.

He tells me of the flooded Bengalis,
refugees year after year,
wave after wave,
each put to work.

As we enter the strait,
Manar points below.

Horizontal turbines
whir on the seafloor bed,
a white-silver blur of curved blades.

An American watches over my shoulder:

 Like the old hand mowers of grass.

Manar answers,
his dark eyes caught in the whirring:

 The triple helix.

Thanks be to Gorlov.

And Darrieus before.

The strait ends.

We enter a bay
wide and shallow.

The turbines of the bay stretch vertical,
reach nearly to the surface of the sea.

The tall turbines spin slower,
each blade clear in its turn.

Dolphins, playful,
chase through the vortex,
slingshot free.

Bodhi

The bay waters brighten
with dawn's golden thaw.

We leave behind
the slow-spinning turbines.

We enter
great hanging gardens
of seaweed -
green,
yellow,
brown.

The seaweed crops pour down
from buoyed ropes in ordered rows.

Their fronds stretch wide.

Their feathered blades
grow thick and tangled.

Their bladder floats
dot stipes like berries.

Manar points to other crops
throughout the gardens:
tiered and netted scallop pens,
dark-shelled mussel towers,
beds of clams and oysters.

We pass small boats
of tending farmers,
hooks and knives in
muscled hands.

We rise to surface
in purple-mossed shallows.

We land on
a pebbled shore.

The gills of the eel angle out.

Fresh air wafts in,
briny, cool.

No one leaves the eel.

We all scan high
the climbing hills.

A city lies
in the rising forest;
colonies link
in a green-patched quilt;
many hundreds of hamlets
tucked and blended.

Manar,
after long gaze,
rushes out through the gill.

Everyone follows
with child eyes wide.

We walk through
a wind-breaking orchard.

An orchard
of the inorganic.

Trees of sapless wood,
waste recycled.

Wide canopy crowns.

Boughs like skeletal fingers
wrapped around orb.

Deep plunging roots.

Thick cabled trunks
carved with the face
of Siddhartha.

The heart-shaped leaves
of the trees harvest wind,
spin round and round
by stiff midrib,
their whir a soft-winged legion.

Manars bows his head to the tree:

The Bodhi fig.

Where Buddha wakened.

We leave the
windy orchard
behind.

We enter calmer airs,
a morning haze, sunlit dew adrift.

A grassy lane
splits twin pools,
still as glass with sky's reflection.

Manar hurries up the lane,
waves us on.

As we follow,
a mountain rises
between the pools.

A mount of human craft,
not plated stone.

A mount with skin
like beech and clay.

From the wide-mounded base,
long shafts stretch high like chimney cluster.

Their broad sides soak up sun.

Roped climbers
swift rappel.

Children wave
from terraced gardens.

Manar waves back:

> *The shafts work both*
> *as mouth and vent.*

> *By ebb and flow*
> *through tunneled web,*
> *the tower breathes*
> *like human lung.*

> *The inner nest stays cool in heat,*
> *warm through winter chill.*

> *All this from termite genius.*

We leave the tower to walk dirt paths
through the waking forest.

Fern leaves fan wide;
branches bend toward sun.

Sundew blankets, pink and green,
tempt flies by sweetened drops.

Mushroom caps glow cobalt blue
in the shade of logs and trunks.

Manar points out
small human homes of woven fiber,
some tucked like nests in tallest trees,
some hanging like cocoons.

We pass geodesic domes
growing mashua, cassava, potatoes,
purple hyacinth, orchids tiger and egret.

We walk the bank of a fast-flowing river,
pause at a spanning bridge half-formed.

An orb flock hovers on the bridge.

By spinneret glands,
the orbs extend converging bridge ends,
printing fluid matrix, depositing light grain.

The bridge-skin,
perforated everywhere
by ellipses long and stretched,
appears as thin as paper.

In seashell imitation,
the bridge
arches,
folds,
and twists.

Manar admires:

> *The open lace of Shi Ling,*
> *stiff by corrugation,*
> *rivals solid steel.*

We follow the river
to a mountain split like hoof.

To gold-misted falls.

Manar welcomes me
to stay here all remaining days:

> *The bitter Andes*
> *gnawed and drained you.*

> *The fierce winds*
> *grinded down.*

> *But, here,*
> *these mild forest hills*
> *will prolong and restore.*

Butterflies

The tired leaders from the eel
sleep through afternoon and night.

They wake at first sun.

They sip yerba tea,
breathe the forest air deep,
exhale slow.

We follow
Chasca and Manar
to a garden tall-hedged
and quiet.

Steaming soup and shellfish wait.

The leaders eat.

The leaders plan.

All are inspired,
impressed by the colony.

All want to send
many refugees here.

But Manar wants to teach,
not absorb.

He wants new colonies
formed on new islands.

He promises guidance and trade.

But he refuses to host.

Australian shippers
warn of pirates and raiders
in the western Atlantic.

A Filipino captain
offers protection in return
for batteries, medicine, fish.

Chasca, concerned,
asks many questions
of the shippers and captain,
keeps open the door.

Manar breaks away
with two eager colonists:
Pakistani and Korean.

Arms over shoulders,
he leads them through the garden.

The leaders remaining
talk of world news.

By a growing consensus,

both AI and human,
the Chilean decoding
has now been confirmed.

The translation
of the alien message
as delivered at Paranal
can be trusted in tone and detail.

Excited,
the leaders imagine
the aliens' homeworld,
their long stellar journey,
the many strange worlds they have seen.

I wander the garden,
alone.

I run my fingers
through thick-bedded moss.

I hold leaves to the light,
trace the veins.

I watch butterflies drift,
flower to flower.

Pappus

At sunset,
Chasca casts a holo
deep among the stars:

A massive comet.

A tail of white dust
scorched and melted.

Disintegrating vapor.

And blue ice boiled dry.

Though shedding constant,
the comet's head does not narrow.

The comet streaks at dazzling speed
but does not leave the sky.

At this sign,
the forest paths soon fill;
the hamlets empty;
thousands gather at the falls.

The water mists climb higher.

Auroral wisps
- jade, bronze, ruby -
quiver through the haze.

A blended voice of many speaks,
announces:

> *New colonies are coming.*

> *Refugees from flood and hunger.*

> *Refugees like us.*

The sky wisps trail away.

The gold haze dims to blue.

Then black.

The crowd sees battered coasts,
villages struck flat,
faces carved by pain.

> *New sisters and new brothers.*

The crowd sees
a rescue ship packed full,
a growing light in weary eyes,
an open island waiting.

The crowd cheers,
claps, whistles.

The sky again falls black.

The cheering fades.

A new face shines in the sky,
an orange-furred mother,
an orangutan in tree.

A sleepy son dozes on her back,
his hands across her neck.

On higher branch,
a wide-cheeked male
calls out across the forest,
enraged, defiant,
as loggers fell the trees.

We tried to save
the last orangutans
still wild.

Through cockpit's eye,
a plane speeds over flattened hills,
fields burnt black, plantations of palm oil.

A slender strip of forest
clings to the distant, rugged mountains.

We did.

Tomorrow,
twenty-six arrive.

Each orangutan is named,
their faces in the sky.

The crowd cheers long and loud.

The sky darkens once more.

The crowd quiets.

The Earth is no longer alone.

The white stars of sky
dissolve into blue.

A sea of blue
with heaving waves.

A sea within seas
in a massive world.

A swift-gusted world
with serpentine cloud chains.

A world without continents,
flecked with myriad islands.

Islands of mountainous coral,
circled by rings of forest marine
and waters abloom with bright algae.

The Addrans have reached out.

Over the ocean world,
a dandelion blossoms in rich floret.

The dandelion ages.

Yellow pales white.

Tufts take to air.

A single pappus sails free.

Beyond triple moons.

Beyond double suns.

Through red-dusted cloud
birthing new stars.

Through deep voids,
gas halos,
starburst shockwaves.

Past ice-rock comets,
dwarf planets,
lobed asteroids.

Toward a small rising star.

To third planet.

To desert by sea.

Mount Paranal.

<u>South</u>

A new holiday is proclaimed:
Addran Eve.

Tonight is the first.

I find the Twins
among the celebrating crowd.

They stand far apart
in a balcony garden.

Brother Okono smiles,
shakes hands, pats shoulders,
whispers new plans to the trusted.

Sister argues,
angry with Manar.

She says
he has inflated hopes,
shared with the people
too much, too soon.

Manar disagrees,
believes that the new hope
will raise humans high,
inspire all Earth.

Men gather to defend him.

Sister, encircled,
walks away,
leaves the garden.

She sees me.

She brightens
and waves.

Together,
we climb the falls
by stairs carved in rock.

At the top,
we look down
to the plunge pools below.

We hear
the party of thousands
over water's hard crash.

Sister speaks,
weary and worn:

And you, Toshiro?

*Do you, too,
disagree?*

Should we answer the Addrans?

Should we welcome them here?

I reach through the rail.

I feel the water's first plunge.

The chill of the water
cuts deep through my fingers.

I savor the chill
and the pain.

I answer:

Who can say?

There are ten-thousand unknowns.

Sister livens,
speaks with her hands:

I see two broad positions,
great danger in both.

If we refuse or ignore
the Addrans' offer to help,
we risk offending potential allies.

We risk a precious opportunity squandered,
billions of lives lost to climate and war.

But if we contact and welcome,
we open a door never to close.

We let in a powerful race who
has traveled the stars.

We kneel down and
open our hands.

I counter with questions:

Can we stop them from coming?
wall off the Earth?

Can we hide?

Can we flee?

Can we find better home?

Sister's face tightens at my words:

So, we broadcast our weakness, our need.

We wait out the century in dizzy expectation.

We hope for the kindness of Empire.

We trust that the Addrans are nothing like ourselves.

This is the plan of Manar and the others.

I take my hand from the water.

Sister takes my wrist, turns,
sees the bare bones of my fingers
under skin threads.

She feels my ears,
my cheeks, my brow.

She tells me that
I am the last of the Novals.

I ask who will follow.

She answers:

Come and see.

Come south with me, Toshiro.

Antarctica waits fierce and wild.

Valientes

We fly low,
beneath the morning fog,
above the ocean waters.

The sun glistens golden
on the tips of the waves,
white on the iceberg faces,
blue on the drifting floes.

Nearing the coast,
the bright ice thickens,
branches,
climbs.

The waters,
deep and dark,
retreat,
narrow into
streams and channels.

Sister banks the mantid.

She turns into a crescent bay.

She follows feeding river.

The river weaves
through cliff-walled mountains,
nearly sheer.

We pass over
petrels in flight,
grey-pebbled banks
with penguins and seals,
bone-picking skuas.

The river ends abruptly
in a glacier of striate tiers -
ice stairs dribbling down.

Tier by tier,
we climb.

We enter a valley
of dry snow dunes.

Sister points to the mount
at the valley's end:

> *There trains*
> *the new generation.*

> *The Valientes.*

> *The Brave.*

We speed through the valley ascending.

Nearing the mount,
Sister brightens and smiles.

She throttles back,
glides in low.

I see the Valientes,
her children,
at the mountain's base.

They run with black wolves,
pull boulders by sleds,
leap crevasses.

Others climb higher
on the mount,
striking ice by the ax,
carving holds,
setting spikes,
digging boots.

A strong gust
sweeps the face,
pelts,
lashes with frost.

The wind-struck climbers
simply dip their heads,
wait out the gust,
climb on.

Many more gather
at the open dome
of the summit.

Braving jets of steam and ash,
harnessed climbers jump into the void.

Sister waves
to her children:

> *After more training*
> *in the sea and desert,*
> *the Valientes will lead*
> *our Crisis Corps.*
>
> *Everywhere disaster strikes,*
> *they will save around the world.*
>
> *The Valientes*
> *will run into the fire,*
> *cover from the storm,*
> *pull life from flood and quake.*

Sister turns for base.

Black

Before
the mantid
touches down
on the white-pearl snow,
the voice of Brother fills.

Brother Okono is angry.

He wants to know
why she left the falls without word,
where she is going, where she has been.

Sister breathes deep.

She silences Brother
with a touch of the panel.

The mantid lands hard,
shakes through its segments.

The thorax opens.

Cold air sweeps in.

Sister leaves quick
as the incoming chill.

I follow her down
the flagged trail to base.

I fix my eyes on her feet.

Her steps are hurried.

Her boots bite the ice,
metal cleats ringing.

I stagger and slip,
unsteady,
club-footed.

Sister draws a green hood.

Barbed flakes of snow
ride the winds,
stick to the green.

I fall behind.

Farther and farther.

The landed flakes
shrink down to specks
of white star.

Sister is gone.

I walk alone.

I see no flags
through the white.

A tongued gust
lifts,
throws me.

My back strikes ice.

Skull into stone.

A black snow falls
from black sky.

<u>Free</u>

I,
Toshiro,
dream through the sea.

The black-watered deep
cannot hold me.

Sister's song
calls me higher.

I break into starlight.

I ride crystal waves.

Sengai cries out
in the breach of the whale.

Ichika smiles
through the silver-mooned mist
of dolphins' wake.

Patient,
free,
we wait for
our children to rise.

Great Thanks

Toshiro Mifune

Dora Maria Tellez

J. E. Williams and Sebastian

Heather and Violet

Jennifer Chikhani

Lindsay Tiry

Luke Danz

Also by Gary David Springer

Coma Dreams

Fuegos

Gabriel

Phera

Fire of Life

Caravaggio's Crossing

Contact

gary_springer@hotmail.com

www.ingramcontent.com/pod-product-compliance
Lightning Source LLC
Chambersburg PA
CBHW040523170726
48295CB00012B/318